JAN BRETT

Daisy Comes Home

SCHOLASTIC INC.

New York   Toronto   London   Auckland   Sydney
Mexico City   New Delhi   Hong Kong   Buenos Aires

*To
Patrick
Zhang Tong
Hearne*

ISBN   0-439-38846-5
Copyright © 2002 by Jan Brett. All rights reserved. Published by Scholastic Inc., 557 Broadway, New York, NY 10012, by arrangement with
G.P. Putnam's Sons, an imprint of Penguin Putnam Books for Young Readers, a division of Penguin Putnam Inc.
SCHOLASTIC and associated logos are trademarks and/or registered trademarks of Scholastic Inc.
12 11 10 9 8 7 6 5 4 3 2 1   3 4 5 6 7 8/0
Printed in the U.S.A.   08
First Scholastic printing, January 2003
Designed by Gunta Alexander. Text set in Hiroshige. The art was done in watercolors and gouache. Airbrush backgrounds by Joseph Hearne.

Look over the garden wall and you will see the six happiest hens in China. They live in Mei Mei's sandy yard by the Li River where they lay brown eggs every day for Mei Mei to sell at the market.

But it was not always this way.

Once upon a time the smallest hen, the one Mei Mei calls Daisy, was picked on by all the others. This is hard to imagine because Mei Mei was known far and wide for her happy hens. She gave them treats. She put fresh hay in their nests. She gave them baths when they fell in black mud. And when she called *Gu-gu-gu-gu!* all the hens would run to her as fast as their legs could carry them.

Even Mei Mei's egg baskets were painted with
big red characters that read "Happy Hens."
And she tried to make it so.

But every night when it was time to roost in the henhouse, the other
hens picked on Daisy. They fluffed up their feathers and crowded her off
the perch. They jostled her until *Peck!* one or the other pushed her and
Thump! off she fell.

Then the hens tucked their heads into their feathers and went to sleep while poor little Daisy was stuck below on the damp mud floor, shivering and cold, until morning.

One day it rained all day and the hens stayed inside. When it got dark, they flew up to their perch—except for Daisy. She had had enough of pushy hens and cold, damp floors. She went outside to find a place to spend the night.

Down on the river bank, she spied one of the market baskets. She snuggled in and fluffed up her feathers to stay warm.

Daisy was sleeping and didn't see the river
creeping up the bank from all the rain. And
when the water reached her Happy Hens
basket, she didn't feel it float out
onto the river.

But when the basket started tipping and bobbing, Daisy woke up. She peeked out and saw a watery world all around her. The sandy yard, the garden wall, and Mei Mei's farmhouse looked smaller and smaller as the current carried her down the river.

Finally the basket bumped against a stone
jetty where a houseboat was tied up. *Scratch,*
scratch, scraped the basket as the river
waves pushed it against the sharp rocks.

A dog was sitting up on the deck of the houseboat. When he saw the
plump hen bobbing in the basket, he barked and scrambled toward her.
Daisy squawked, and pecked, and beat the air with her wings.
It was enough to tip the basket off the rocks and
she floated away just in time.

Dawn broke over the Gui Mountains as the basket
drifted along the river. Branches brushed against it.
Fish swam silently by and birds flew overhead.
Suddenly Daisy felt a *thump*.

Daisy looked up and saw two big horns and a pair of surprised eyes looking
down at her. The basket had drifted into the legs of a great big water buffalo taking
a morning drink. The buffalo snorted loudly, scaring Daisy. She flew forward and
nipped his furry muzzle and flapped and flapped her wings.

Daisy scared the water buffalo! He turned and galloped up the bank, scattering the ducks as he ran. His splashes made waves that carried the basket back into the middle of the river.

Daisy traveled along all day until her basket was hooked by the roots of a banyan tree where a troop of red-tailed monkeys lived. The curious monkeys eyed Daisy and climbed down for a closer look. Daisy froze as one monkey crept up to the basket and reached in.

Daisy flapped and pecked, nipped and squawked.
The startled monkey pushed the basket away. It broke
loose from the tree and floated on down the river.
Daisy wondered what would happen next.

Up ahead Daisy saw a fisherman with cormorants diving all around his bamboo boat. They were catching fish and taking them to him for a reward. The fisherman felt a soft *bump* behind him. Thinking it was a cormorant, he reached back and grabbed. How surprised he was to see that he was holding a hen instead of a cormorant!

"Finders keepers," he exclaimed. "Little fish, big fish, silver fish, white fish. That's what I sell at the market. But today I will have this tender young chicken!" He put a net over the basket and headed to shore with poor Daisy inside.

At home Mei Mei had looked all day and all night for her little Daisy. She wasn't in the henhouse. She wasn't behind the farmhouse. She couldn't fly over the wall. *Where is she?* Mei Mei wondered, worried all the time about what had happened to Daisy. Finally she knew that she had to go to the market. With a sad feeling, she packed her eggs in their baskets and started on her way.

As the baskets swung back and forth, the red characters on the sides of her baskets made Mei Mei feel sadder and sadder. "Happy Hens," she said aloud to herself. "What about my Daisy. Where can she be?"

At the market, Mei Mei found a place and arranged the eggs in clean, sweet-smelling straw. All morning, shoppers bought her fresh brown eggs. But she couldn't stop thinking about her little lost hen.

Mei Mei heard a voice calling to her. It was her friend Zhang yelling from the back of a bike-cart. "A fisherman has a Happy Hens basket," he shouted.

"What?" she called, not understanding what he
was saying.

"A Happy Hens basket," he repeated. "You'd better
hurry because he's showing off what's inside."

"Daisy!" Mei Mei shouted.

Mei Mei raced to where the fish were sold. There was Daisy, beautiful and plump in her basket, surrounded by a crowd, all wanting to buy her.

"That's my hen!" she cried to the fisherman. But his face was like stone. She pointed to the red characters on the basket. "Happy Hens," she said. The fisherman crossed his arms. "Finders keepers!" he growled and turned away to sell Daisy.

Mei Mei was about to leave, but her eyes rested
[on] those characters, "Happy Hens." All she could
[thi]nk about was Daisy in a cooking pot. She
[squ]eezed her eyes shut and clenched her fists.
[Sh]e had to do something!

"*Gu-gu-gu-gu-gu!*" she called at the top of her voice. And when Daisy heard that call, she answered it the way she had every day of her life. She rose up and threw herself against the basket, tipping it over. She ran toward her friend Mei Mei as fast as her legs could go.

Daisy flew onto Mei Mei's shoulder and off they went, running back to get Mei Mei's baskets and go home.

The fisherman ran after them, furious. "Stop," he yelled at Mei Mei.

"That's *my* hen!"

"Finders keepers!" Mei Mei called over her shoulder.

And with Daisy clinging to her, she ran and didn't stop until they were safely home.

That night, as the sun went down, Daisy took a place on the roost. When one of the big hens fluffed up her wings and spread out, expecting Daisy to fall off the perch like always, Daisy flapped her wings. "I learned that from a boat dog," she clucked. Another hen tried to tip her off. She pushed right back. "I scared a water buffalo like that," she squawked. Another hen jostled her. *Peck! Peck!*

Peck! Peck! Daisy kept her place on the perch and
beat the air with her wings. She remembered the
monkey and she pecked and flapped all over
again. That was when the hens gave Daisy
a place of her own.

The *lap, lap, lap* of the river made a peaceful nighttime song.
No bumping, no jostling, no fussing around—just six happy hens,
their heads tucked in their feathers, high and warm and safe, together.